Ghostyshocks ☆ Snow White ☆ Cinderboy ☆ Eco-Wolf ☆
The Greedy Farmer ☆ Billy Beast ☆

LITTLE RED RIDING WOLF

Written by Laurence Anholt
Illustrated by Arthur Robins

ORCHARD BOOKS
96 Leonard Street, London EC2A 4XD
Orchard Books Australia
32/45-51 Huntley Street, Alexandria, NSW 2015
First published in Great Britain in 1998. This edition published in 2002.
Text © Laurence Anholt 1998. Illustrations © Arthur Robins 1998.
The rights of Laurence Anholt to be identified as the author
and Arthur Robins as the illustrator of this work
have been asserted by them in accordance with the
Copyright, Designs and Patents Act, 1988.
A CIP catalogue record for this book is available from the British Library.
ISBN 1 84121 400 0
3 5 7 9 10 8 6 4 2
Printed in China

ORCHARD BOOKS

☆ The Fried Piper ☆ Shampoozel ☆ Daft Jack ☆ The Emperor
☆ Little Red Riding Wolf ☆ Rumply Crumply Stinky Pin

In the very darkest corner of the deep dark wood sat the Big Bad Girl.

The Big Bad Girl was just about as
BIG and BAD as a girl can be, and all
the woodland animals were afraid of her.

She hung about beside the forest path and carved her name on trees. She shouted rude things at any little animal who passed by.

The Big Bad Girl tripped up little deer. She stole fir cones from baby squirrels and threw them at the poor little hedgehogs. The woodland birds didn't dare to sing when the Big Bad Girl was around!

But the person the Big Bad Girl liked to tease most of all was a charming little wolf cub who often passed by on his way to visit his dear old granny wolf.

Little Wolfie was the sweetest, fluffiest, politest little cub you could ever hope to meet. He would run along the path, *skippety-skip*, carrying a basket of freshly baked goodies for Old Granny Wolf, singing all the time…

"I'm a little wolfie, good and sweet
I am tidy, I am neat.
With a basket full of lovely grub,
I am Granny's favourite cub."

"Wot's in yer basket today, Little-Weedy-Wolfie-Wimp?" snarled the Big Bad Girl. "Mmmm, apple pies? I'll take those. Jam sandwiches? Very tasty."

"Oh dear, oh dear! Now there will be nothing for dear Old Granny Wolf," wailed Little Wolfie. And his little wolfie tears rolled into the empty basket.

Now, the Big Bad Girl's father was not big and bad at all. He was a kind old hat-maker who loved hats in every shape and size, and thought everyone should wear one night and day.

But the sad truth was, his hats were so awful that nobody would buy them. He had only sold one nightcap in his entire life, and the family was terribly poor.

"I can't understand it," he sighed. "I make these marvellous hats from dawn till dusk until my fingers are worn to the bone, but even my own daughter will not wear them. Please, my dear," he begged, "wear this one for me."

"Father," answered the appalling child,
"I would rather wear one of your old socks
on my head than this hat. Why can't you get
a decent job? Nobody is a hat-maker these
days. Couldn't you be a woodcutter like
other people's dads?"

The Big Bad Girl hated hats so much that as soon as her father gave her a new one, she would run into the woods and give it to a baby badger or a little squirrel to wear, whether they liked it or not.

Then, to her father's dismay, she would return home, bare-headed, pretending she had lost the hat in the forest.

One day, however, the Big Bad Girl's father made her a hat that was more ridiculous than anything he had made before. This one was a real monster. It was bright red with a woolly

bobble on top, little flaps over the ears and dangly bows to tie under the chin. It even had a small red cape to match. The old man was delighted with his creation. "Surely my daughter will LOVE this one," he laughed, jumping up and down with excitement.

But the Big Bad Girl said, "Father, you have made some vile things in your life, but this hat is THE PITS! I would rather wear your old underpants on my head. You have as much fashion sense as a dung-beetle!"

As her father lay weeping in his workshop, the Big Bad Girl stomped into the forest to find some unsuspecting little animal to wear the red riding hat.

But, alas, this one was so awful that no
one would touch it. Even the Woodland
Oxfam shop sent her away.

The Big Bad Girl sat by the forest path wondering what to do.

"Surely someone will be stupid enough to wear this hat," she said. As she spoke, she heard a delightful little song…

BIG BAD GIRL

And who should come along the path, *skippety-skip*, but Little Wolfie.

"Ah, ha!" sniggered the Big Bad Girl. "Here comes Creepy-Cutesy-Custard-Cub. My red riding hat would suit him perfectly! I will trick him into wearing it. Then I will make fun of him FOREVER! Heh heh heh!"

"Where are you going, Little Fluffy Flea Face?" growled the Big Bad Girl.

"I am off to visit my darling old granny wolf," replied Little Wolfie, politely.

"Well, I have just seen yer old granny wolf," lied the rotten girl. "You can't see her today because she is poorly and might give you her old granny wolf germs."

"Oh, poor Old Granny Wolf," sighed Little Wolfie, sadly.

"But," continued the wicked girl, "she has made you a lovely sort of hat thing. She told me to give it to you and tell you never to take it off, night or day, even if people laugh at you."

Little Wolfie was very pleased…

...until he saw the revolting red riding hat. Then even he had doubts.

But being a good little chap and wanting
to please his granny, he tied it on his fluffy
little head with the dangly ribbons.

The Big Bad Girl almost choked with laughter.

Holy Sweaty Snake Socks! she thought. This little wolf is UNBELIEVABLY stupid.

But Little Red Riding Wolf said 'thank you' politely and set off home, *skippety-skip*, chattering away to himself.

"How pleased I am with my new riding hat that Granny has made me. From now on I will call myself *Little Red Riding Wolf*. That will please her even more."

The Big Bad Girl rolled on the path and roared with laughter. "Holy Newt's Knickers! LITTLE RED RIDING WOLF!! What a name! A wolf should be called *Hairy Howler* or *Bone Cruncher* or *Old Yellow Eyes*. Little Red Riding Wolf is a TERRIBLE name."

All that day, Little Wolfie wore the red riding hat and tried not to notice when people laughed at him.

The next morning he said to himself, "Surely my dear old granny wolf will be better today. I will run along the path and show her how pleased I am with my lovely hat." And off he went, *skippety-skip...*

"I'm a little wolfie, so polite,
I am brave, I am bright.

I am happy, I am good,
In my new red riding hood."

BUT, by the side of the path, in the middle of the deep dark wood, blowing bubbles with her gum, something REALLY NASTY was waiting for him…

"I am not Tomato Head," said Little Red Riding Wolf, fighting back the tears. "I am Little Red Riding Wolf."

"Where are you going, Ketchup Cap?" demanded the Big Bad Girl, wiping her filthy nose on the back of her hand.

"I am going to dear Old Granny Wolf's house to see if she is better and to thank her for this lovely hat. Now, excuse me while I fill my basket with these pretty spring flowers for her kitchen table."

While Little Red Riding Wolf picked his flowers, the Big Bad Girl picked her nose thoughtfully. "That wrinkly Old Granny Wolf will spoil my fun," she said to herself. "I will take a shortcut to her house. If she gives me any trouble, I will lock her in the cupboard, then I will pretend that I am Old Granny Wolf. I bet she is even smaller and weedier than little Strawberry Top."

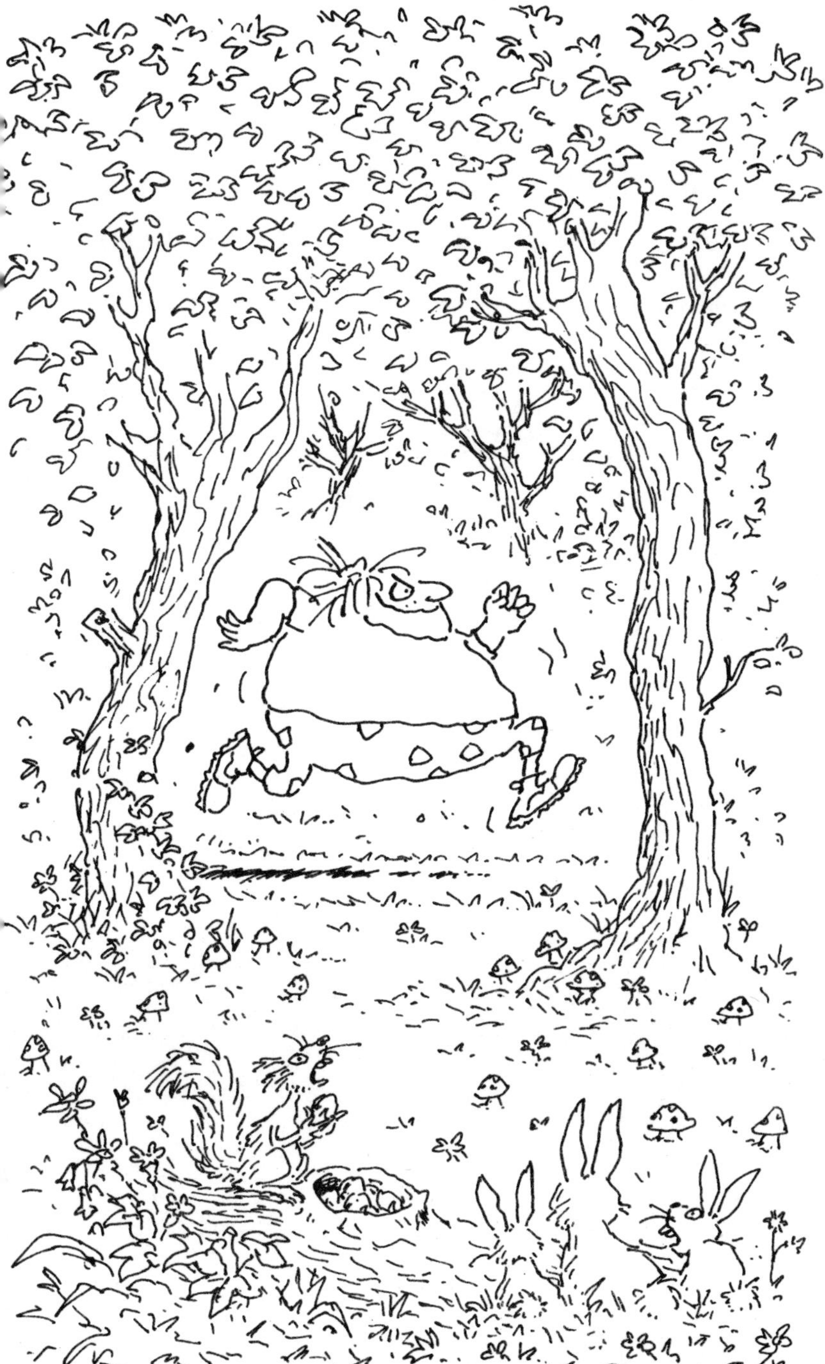

So the Big Bad Girl ran as quickly as she could to Old Granny Wolf's house. It was a very big house for a little old granny wolf.

But Old Granny Wolf was out chopping wood in the forest.

The Big Bad Girl climbed in the back
window and ran indoors, just as Little Red
Riding Wolf tapped at the door.

"Old Granny Wolf, Old Granny Wolf. It
is I, Little Red Riding Wolf, in my brand
new hat."

"Holy Hopping Hedgehog Droppings!
That was quick," said the Big Bad Girl.
She ran up the stairs and searched for
somewhere to hide. She noticed a huge
bed, but how could she make herself look
like an old granny wolf?

On a hook on the back of the door, the Big Bad Girl found Old Granny Wolf's pink lacy nightcap. Little Wolfie had bought it for Old Granny Wolf's birthday, but she never really wore it. Of course, the Big Bad Girl HATED hats – and this one was even worse than the red riding hat.

But the Big Bad Girl had no choice. She pulled the ghastly nightcap right down to her eyes and climbed into the bed, just as Little Red Riding Wolf came running up the stairs, *skippety-skip*.

"Old Granny Wolf, Old Granny Wolf. Where are you?" he called.

"Er, over 'ere, Little Woolly Hood Head," answered the Big Bad Girl.

"Oh Old Granny Wolf, Old Granny Wolf, thank you for the beautiful hat you made me. Doesn't it look wonderful?"

"Er…yeah, Little Bobble Brain…really wicked," replied the Big Bad Girl.

"But Old Granny Wolf, Old Granny Wolf, what a tiny voice you have and what small teeth you have too. Perhaps you are still poorly. You seem so pale and weedy today."

"Listen, Little Jam Man. You should learn not to make personal remarks!" snapped the Big Bad Girl.

"But Old Granny Wolf, Old Granny Wolf what small ears you have. In fact...I don't think you are my old granny wolf at all. She is MUCH bigger than you."

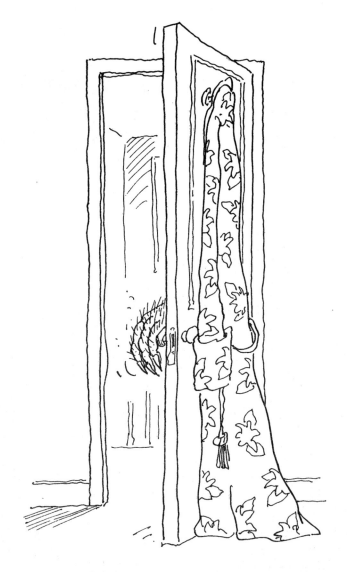

At that precise moment Old Granny Wolf
pushed open the door...

Old Granny Wolf was ENORMOUS.
She had huge yellow eyes,
big sharp teeth and
a long dribbly tongue.
She was carrying a
great sharp axe.

"Ah, Little Wolfie," she said. "What a nice surprise. You are just in time for tea. But why are you wearing that ridiculous hat? And what is this thing in my bed? It looks like a Big Bad Girl – a very tasty Big Bad Girl – just right for my BIG BAD TEA!"

The Big Bad Girl leapt out of bed, down the stairs, out of the door, into the forest and along the path as fast as her big bad legs would carry her. She hammered on her father's door.

"Father, Father," yelled the Big Bad Girl.
"Let me in. Let me in. I will be good. I will
do whatever you ask."

Her father peeped out of the window. He couldn't believe what he was seeing. There was his daughter wearing a delightful nightcap. It reminded him of one he had made himself many years before... He remembered it well because it was the only one he had ever sold.

"I will let you in," he said. "But only if you promise to wear a hat night and day – the one you are wearing now suits you beautifully!"

And so from that day on, the Big Bad Girl became a Big Good Girl (for most of the time). She found a job as a woodcutter, and her boss kept a very careful, big yellow eye on her.

The Big Good Girl kept her promise to
wear a hat every day, although it was usually
a chainsaw helmet.

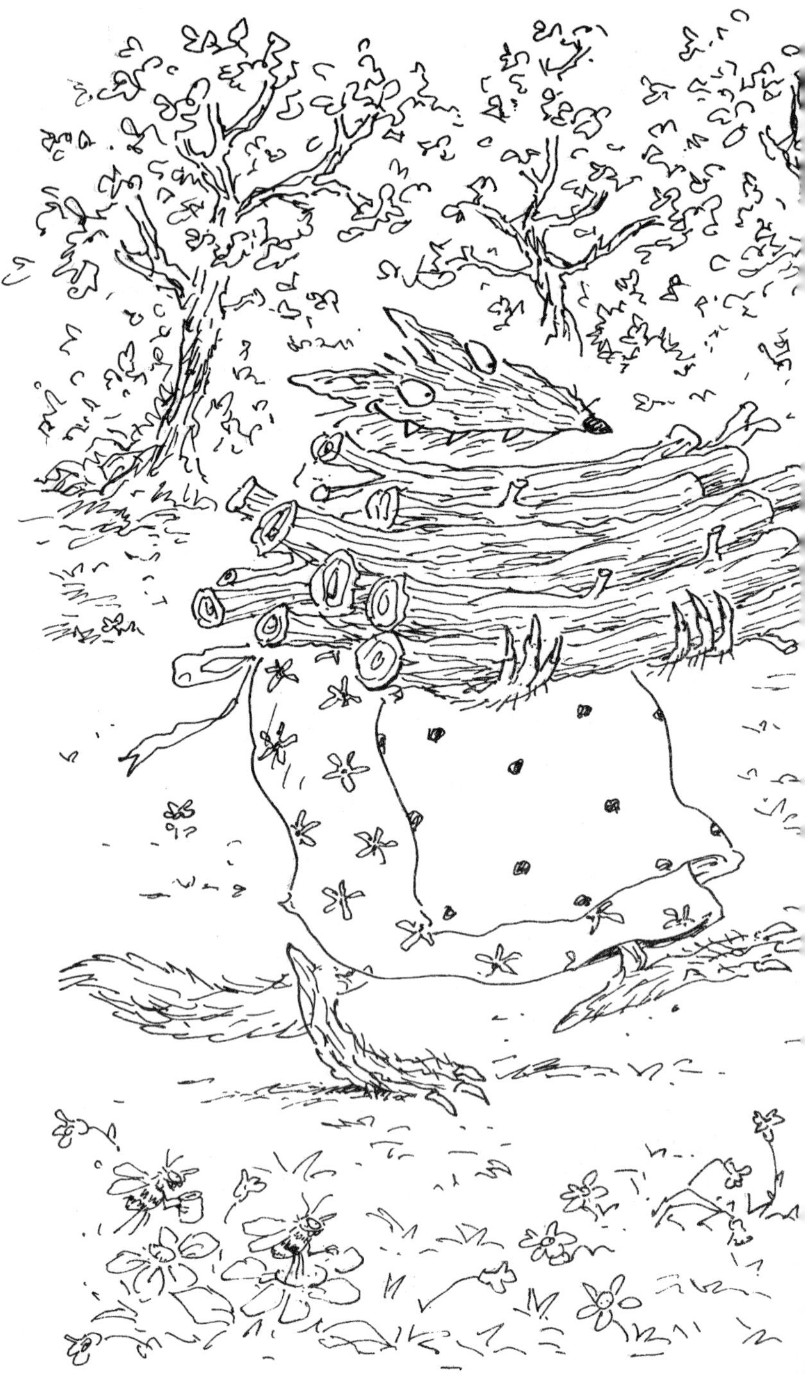

And the red riding hat was useful…

…when they had an especially heavy load.